Ken Wilson-Max

Where's Lenny?

Alanna Max

There goes Lenny,
playing hide and seek.

Here's Daddy, counting and singing...

Daddy counts.

"1 2 3 4 5

Once I caught a fish alive.

6 7 8 9 10

Then I let it go again."

“Ready or not, here I come!”

Where's Lenny?

Daddy hears a rumbling
in the cupboard.

"Aha!" he says.
But when he opens
the door he finds nothing.

Where's Lenny?

Daddy sniffs
and follows his nose
to the living room.

“Aha!” he says.
But it’s only Mummy
eating toast.

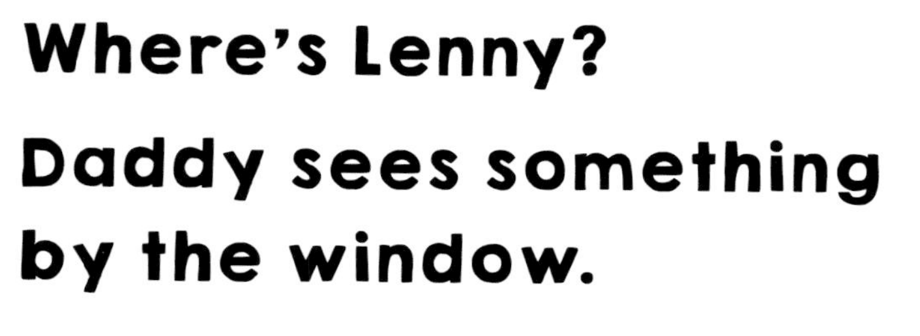

Where's Lenny?

Daddy sees something
by the window.

"Aha!" he says.
But it's only Wilbur
wagging his tail.

Where's Lenny?

Daddy hears a bubbling noise, but it's only Gordon the goldfish.

Where's Lenny?

Daddy sees blobs of jam
and follows them
up the stairs.

Where's Lenny?

Daddy hears tap, tap, tap
in the bathroom.

"Aha!" he says.
But it's only Mummy,
fixing the light.

Where's Lenny?

Mummy and Daddy rush into Lenny's room.

"Aha!"
they say.
But no-one
is there.

Then they hear a giggle.

Mummy and Daddy creep towards the little giggly bump in the bed and...

“Aha!” says Daddy.

Here's Lenny!

Here are
Mummy and Daddy
with Lenny,

tickling and tickling,
laughing and hugging.